GHOSTS

RAINA TELGEMEIER

GHOSTS

WITH COLOR BY BRADEN LAMB

graphix

An Imprint of

SCHOLASTIC

All rights reserved. Published by Graphix, an imprint of Scholastic Inc.,
Publishers since 1920. SCHOLASTIC, GRAPHIX, and associated logos are
trademarks and/or registered trademarks of Scholastic Inc.

The publisher does not have any control over and does not assume any
responsibility for author or third-party websites or their content.

Library of Congress Cataloging-in-Publication Data

Names: Telgemeier, Raina, author, illustrator.
Title: Ghosts / Raina Telgemeier ; with color by Braden Lamb.
Description: First edition. | New York : Graphix, an imprint of Scholastic, 2016. | © 2016 |
Summary: Catrina and her family have moved to the coast of Northern California for the sake
of her little sister, Maya, who has cystic fibrosis—and Cat is even less happy about the move when
she is told that her new town is inhabited by ghosts, and Maya sets her heart on meeting one.
Identifiers: LCCN 2016004672 | ISBN 9780545540612 (hc) | ISBN 9780545540629 (pb)
Subjects: LCSH: Sisters—Comic books, strips, etc. | Sisters—Juvenile fiction. | Ghosts—Comic books,
strips, etc. | Ghost stories. | Moving, Household—Comic books, strips, etc. | Moving, Household—
Juvenile fiction. | Families—California, Northern—Comic books, strips, etc. | Families—California,
Northern—Juvenile fiction. | California, Northern—Comic books, strips, etc. | California, Northern—
Juvenile fiction. | CYAC: Graphic novels. | Sisters—Fiction. | Ghosts—Fiction. |
Cystic fibrosis—Fiction. | Moving, Household—Fiction. | Family life—Fiction. | California,
Northern—Fiction. Classification: LCC PZ7.7.T45 Gh 2016 | DDC 741.5/973—dc23
LC record available at http://lccn.loc.gov/2016004672

14 13 12   19 20 21

Printed in China   62
First edition, September 2016
Edited by Cassandra Pelham
Lettering by Jenny Staley
Book design by Phil Falco
Creative Director: David Saylor

FOR SABINA

1

4

6

12

13

16

crunch   crunch

39

43

Poke
Poke
jiggle

SO WHAT ARE THE GHOSTS LIKE?

SOME, LIKE MY BROTHER JOSÉ, AREN'T TOO DIFFERENT FROM WHEN THEY WERE ALIVE.

BECAUSE OF THE, UM, **ACCOMMODATING** WEATHER IN THIS TOWN . . .

YOU MEAN THE FOG?

YES. BECAUSE OF THE FOG, THE GHOSTS SEE OUR TOWN AS THE PERFECT PLACE TO HANG OUT.

49

*AN ALTAR FOR A DECEASED RELATIVE

67

MAYA'S GOING TO BE AMAZED WHEN I TELL HER I SAW A --

111

127

WHAT ARE YOU DOING HERE?

131

137

138

SLAM!

149

DING DONG...

159

175

188

TINK

199

HEYYY!
GOOD TO
SEE YOU,
NEIGHBORS!

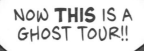

NOW **THIS** IS A GHOST TOUR!!

Hee hee...

A FEW NOTES ABOUT
GHOSTS

BAHÍA DE LA LUNA

Bahía de la Luna was inspired by foggy coastal Northern California, where I grew up. I've always had an appreciation for the windswept coastline, the gnarly cypress trees, and especially the seaside town of Half Moon Bay, which is famous for its artichoke fields, pumpkin farms, and cheerful, laid-back Halloween vibe. I wanted Bahía de la Luna to feel like that, and the characters who live there to reflect the laid-back, gnarly, slightly haunted atmosphere.

DÍA DE LOS MUERTOS

Día de los Muertos, or Day of the Dead, is an ancient tradition that is now largely celebrated in Mexico and throughout the world. Instead of mourning the loss of loved ones, Mexican culture chooses to celebrate and honor the dead each year at the beginning of November, building altars (ofrendas) in homes, parks, and cemeteries, and decorating them with flowers, food, photographs, and other personal items. Although Day of the Dead represents the afterlife, there is something undeniably joyous about it!

I was very fortunate to attend San Francisco's annual Day of the Dead celebration during the course of creating this book. Thousands of people came together to dress up, build altars, light candles, and remember their loved ones. It was one of the most beautiful, respectful, and moving experiences I've ever had. Many of the visuals from the celebration scene in *Ghosts* came directly from that night, as I sat, sketched, and observed everything and everyone around me. The process of creating a book is not unlike letting go of the things that haunt your past. Making peace with your ghosts is as profound as the idea of life itself. And at the end of the day, love transcends life and death.

CYSTIC FIBROSIS

Cystic fibrosis is a genetic disease that causes thick, sticky mucus to build up in the lungs, making breathing difficult and leading to frequent infections. Some of the treatments Maya endures in this story are the vibrating vest designed to break up the mucus in her lungs (making it easier to cough out); extra nutrition delivered through a port in her belly while she sleeps; and, eventually, a breathing tube to administer more oxygen. Scar tissue can build up in the lungs following infections, reducing the space available for air to pass through. In some cases, CF patients need to undergo lung transplants. While there is no cure, improved treatments for CF have greatly extended the life expectancy of patients. I chose to write about cystic fibrosis because breathing is a huge theme in this story. Ghosts can't breathe, and Maya can't breathe very well herself. Cat has normal lungs, but she is often anxious and sometimes needs to be reminded to stop and breathe deeply. You can learn more about cystic fibrosis at www.cff.org.

SKETCHBOOK

These sketches were done in 2008, eight years before the publication of *Ghosts*! The characters, their story, and this environment have existed in my head for a very long time.

THANK

This book drew a lot of inspiration from my cousin Sabina Castello Collado, whom we lost to cancer when she was thirteen. Sabina was one of the most inspiring kids I ever met: spirited, joyful, and not interested in letting her illness define her or slow her down. She is greatly missed and will never be forgotten.

Sabina's parents, Suzanne and Dioni, and her siblings, Sophia and Adonis, also blew me away with the depth of their love for their daughter and sister. They are incredible people and I wish to thank them for everything they are and everything they do. Special thanks to Sophia for being one of the coolest big sisters I've ever known.

Thanks to Dave Roman and the Cuevas, Roman, Rigores, and Fernandez families for their support. Special thanks to Tammy Diaz Cuevas for talking tamales with me.

The cystic fibrosis community, especially the brave families who posted their stories online, was a constant source of inspiration as well as a great resource for understanding.

My editors, Cassandra Pelham and David Saylor, nurtured this project from the ground up and helped me down the winding path that leads from one ocean to another. I can't think of two better people with whom to wander the windy hillside that is creating graphic novels.

Thanks to Phil Falco, Sheila Marie Everett, Lizette Serrano, Tracy van Straaten, Lori Benton, Ellie Berger, Bess Braswell, Antonio Gonzalez, Caitlin Friedman, Michelle Campbell, Emily Heddleson, and the rest of the incredible team at Scholastic. I love working with all of you.

Braden Lamb deserves an extra-special round of bone-rattling applause for the coloring of my art for this book, translating my notes and reference for the atmosphere of Bahía de la Luna into stunning Technicolor. And muchas gracias to Braden's team of assistants, Shelli Paroline and Rachel Maguire!

Additional thanks to my studio assistants, Alexandra Graudins and Kristen Adam, for providing so much help, never-ending good cheer, and cookies; my wonder agent, Judy Hansen; ace letterer Jenny Staley; Sofia Vasquez-Duran, for talking health and medicine; Jewels Green, for her thoughtful insights on cystic fibrosis; and my friend in all things art, introspection, and skeletons, Ashley Despain.

Thanks to the authors, artists, filmmakers, and photographers who inspired me to think about spirits and magical realism and history and delicious food. Thanks to the librarians, booksellers, teachers, comics community, and everyone who has supported my work so wholeheartedly. Thanks to the state of California, my lifelong muse. Thanks to my family, who don't seem to mind living in the fog; I'll bear it if I have to, as long as you guys are here. Thanks to my friends, who are a continual source of love, support, and ideas. I'd be lost in the dark without them.

Finally, an orange soda toast to my readers, young and old, who are endlessly amazing.

—Raina

BIBLIOGRAPHY

While *Ghosts* is a work of fiction, I conducted many interviews with friends and family members, and referenced or participated in the following resources during the creation of this book.

BOOKS

Carmichael, Elizabeth and Chloë Sayer. *The Skeleton at the Feast: The Day of the Dead in Mexico.* Austin: University of Texas Press, 1991.

Greenleigh, John and Rosalind Rosoff Beimler. *The Days of the Dead: Mexico's Festival of Communion with the Departed.* Portland: Pomegranate Communications, 1998.

Hyams, Gina and Masako Takahashi. Day of the Dead Box. San Francisco: Chronicle Books, 2001.

Stavans, Ilan, ed. *Wáchale! Poetry and Prose about Growing Up Latino in America.* Chicago: Cricket Books, 2001.

Tonatiuh, Duncan. *Funny Bones: Posada and His Day of the Dead Calaveras.* New York: Abrams Books for Young Readers, 2015.

Winningham, Geoff, Richard Rodriguez, and J. M. G. Le Clézio. *In the Eye of the Sun: Mexican Fiestas.* New York: W. W. Norton & Company, 1996.

ARTICLES

Delsol, Christine. "La Catrina: Mexico's Grand Dame of Death." *SFGate.* October 25, 2011. http://www.sfgate.com/mexico/mexicomix/article/La-Catrina-Mexico-s-grande-dame-of-death-2318009.php#photo-1824635

Gawande, Atul. "The Bell Curve." *The New Yorker.* December 6, 2004. http://www.newyorker.com/magazine/2004/12/06/the-bell-curve

Trivedi, Bijal P. "Doorway to a Cure for Cystic Fibrosis." *Discover.* July 30, 2013. http://discovermagazine.com/2013/september/14-doorway-to-a-cure

Wineland, Claire. "Living Life from a Hospital Room." CNN. October 23, 2014. http://www.cnn.com/2014/10/23/health/cystic-fibrosis-clairity-project/

WEBSITES

Cystic Fibrosis Foundation: www.cff.org
Day of the Dead in Mexico: www.dayofthedead.com
The Marigold Project: www.dayofthedeadsf.org
Mexican Sugar Skull: www.mexicansugarskull.com
SOMArts: www.somarts.org

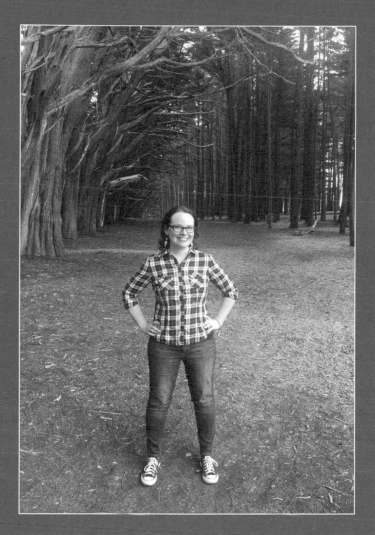

RAINA TELGEMEIER is the #1 *New York Times* bestselling, multiple Eisner Award–winning creator of *Smile* and *Sisters*, which are both graphic memoirs based on her childhood. She is also the creator of *Drama*, which was named a Stonewall Honor Book and was selected for YALSA's Top Ten Great Graphic Novels for Teens. Raina lives in the San Francisco Bay Area. To learn more, visit her online at www.goRaina.com.

ALSO BY
RAINA TELGEMEIER